HENRY and MUDGE

AND THE
Careful Cousin

The Thirteenth Book of Their Adventures

Story by Cynthia Rylant
Pictures by Suçie Stevenson

SCHOLASTIC INC.

New York Toronto London Auckland Sydney
Mexico City New Delhi Hong Kong Buenos Aires

To Henry Seltzer, Jr.—another great Henry—CR

For my own careful cousin, Sue Plant—SS

ISBN 0-590-98244-3

Text copyright © 1994 by Cynthia Rylant.
Illustrations copyright © 1994 by Suçie Stevenson.
All rights reserved.
Published by Scholastic Inc., 557 Broadway, New York, NY 10012,
by arrangement with Simon & Schuster Books for Young Readers,
Simon & Schuster Children's Publishing Division.
SCHOLASTIC and associated logos are trademarks and/or
registered trademarks of Scholastic Inc.

12 11 10 9 8 7 6 5 4 3   4 5 6 7 8/0

Printed in the U.S.A.   23

First Scholastic printing, September 2003

The text of this book is set in 18-point Goudy Old Style.
The illustrations are pen-and-ink and watercolor,
reproduced in full color.
Cover redesigned by Christopher A. Motil.

Contents

Watching for Annie

One day Henry and his
big dog Mudge were standing on their
front porch, watching the road.
They were watching for Henry's cousin.
"Her name is Annie," Henry told Mudge,
"and she's spending the night."

Mudge scratched an ear.

"I've never met her," Henry said.

Mudge chewed a foot.

"I sure hope she's fun,"
Henry said.

Mudge stretched some bones.

While they waited for the cousin
Henry gave Mudge a brushing.
Mudge loved brushings.
He rolled onto his back.
He hung his paws in the air.
He closed his eyes and made
little dog-grunts.
Mudge *loved* brushings.
And they made him look very
nice for company.

Suddenly a car pulled into
Henry's driveway.
"Up, Mudge," said Henry. "She's here."
Mudge jumped up.
He wagged his tail.

He barked a little bark.

He danced a little dance.
Mudge loved company.

A tall man got out of the car.

"Hello, Henry!" he called.

"Hello, Uncle Ed!" Henry called back.

A girl got out of the car.

"Hello, Henry!" she called.

"Hello, Annie!" Henry called back.

She sure looks dressed up,
Henry thought.
She sure looks clean,
he thought.
Uh-oh, he thought.
Annie stood in the yard.
Her dress was frilly.
Her shoes were shiny.
Her face was worried.

"Does he bite?" Annie asked,
pointing to Mudge.
"Oh, no," said Henry.
Mudge wagged his tail.

"Does he jump on people?" she asked.
"Not anymore," said Henry.
Mudge kept wagging.

"Does he *drool?*" Annie asked.

Henry looked at Mudge.

Mudge looked at Henry.

"Well . . ." Henry said.

He looked at Annie's nice frilly dress.

He looked at Annie's nice shiny shoes.

Henry looked at the drool on his front porch.

Uh-oh, he thought.

It was The Visit of the Careful Cousin.

Annie Turns Pink

Henry made Mudge sit while
Annie went into the house.
Mudge wagged his tail and drooled
on the porch as she walked by.
Then he followed Henry inside.

Annie was on the couch.

Before Henry could say no,

Mudge went over and kissed Annie

on the face.

Annie turned pink.

She opened her shiny purse
and pulled out a hanky.
She wiped the dog drool
from her cheeks.
She did not look happy.

"No more kisses, Mudge," Annie said.
"No more kisses, Mudge," Henry said,
even though Henry could not believe
a person would not like dog kisses.

He could not believe this girl
was really his cousin.
He could not believe she would be
here a whole day and night.

"Want to see my fish?" he asked her.

Maybe she likes fish, he thought.

Fish don't drool.

Annie picked up her purse.

She followed Henry, and Mudge

followed her.

Henry had forgotten about the baseball cards.

And the empty cracker boxes.

And the dirty socks.

At the door of Henry's room,
Annie's eyes got wide, and
her mouth hung open.
Uh-oh, thought Henry.
But suddenly Annie smiled.
"Fish!" she said.

She walked over to the fish tank.

She put her head near the water.

She grabbed her nose.

"Yuck," she said. "It smells."

"Fish always smell," said Henry.

"They smell like fish."

He wondered what Annie would do if she ever smelled Mudge's mouth.

Annie sat on Henry's bed.
"What do you do for fun?"
she asked Henry.
"I play with Mudge," Henry said.

"What do you do?"
"I play the piano," said Annie.
Henry wondered why someone would want
to play with a piano instead of a dog.

"Do you like fudge cookies?" Henry asked.
He thought maybe they could just eat
while Annie visited.

"I *love* fudge cookies," said Annie.

"Great!" said Henry.

Mudge was wagging.

He loved fudge cookies, too.

Henry felt around under his bed.
He pulled out a brown paper bag.
It had some dust balls on it
and an old piece of hard gum
stuck under it.

Henry pulled out a cookie and handed
it to Annie.

She turned pink again.

Uh-oh, thought Henry.

This was going to be a very long visit.

Zam!

Henry and Annie were eating lunch
with Uncle Ed and Henry's parents.
"So, Annie, did you see Henry's room?"
asked Uncle Ed.
Annie nodded.

"Did you pet his dog?"

Annie nodded again.

"Did you watch his fish?"

Annie nodded one more time.

Henry worried.

What if Annie talked about
the dog drool
and the smelly tank
and the dusty cookies?
Henry's parents would feel bad.
Especially Henry's dad.
He was even messier than Henry.
His car had a million hamburger
wrappers on the floor.

But Annie didn't say
anything bad.
She didn't say anything at all.
She just cut up her hot dog into
tiny pieces and ate quietly.

Henry had not given up.

There must be something they could
do together.

"Do you play Frisbee?" he asked Annie.

"No." Annie shook her head.

"Want to try?" Henry asked.

Annie thought for a minute.

She nodded her head.

"Great!" said Henry.

Outside, Henry stood on one
side of the yard and
Annie stood on the other.
Mudge stayed in the middle
so he could run both ways.
He was pretty good at Frisbee
except that he got the Frisbee all wet.

Henry told Annie how to make
the Frisbee spin.
He told her not to worry.
He told her it takes a while
to get good at Frisbee.
Then he told her to throw the
Frisbee to him.

ZAM!

The Frisbee whizzed across the yard
and into Henry's hands like a rocket.

"Wow!" said Henry.

"Wow!" said Annie.

She looked at her hand as if
she didn't believe it
belonged to her.

Henry whizzed a slow one back.

Annie shot it back to Henry.

ZAM!

"Wow!" they both said again.

They played Frisbee all afternoon.

Annie was really good.

At first she stopped a lot

to dry off the Frisbee after

Mudge got it.

But pretty soon she got used to dog drool and threw the wet Frisbee anyway.

After supper Henry and Mudge and Annie
played Frisbee again until dark.

Then they went inside to Henry's room.

They were sweaty and dirty and tired.

They were hungry, too.

Henry said he would go to the kitchen

for a bag of cookies.

"Oh, no," said Annie.

She pulled the brown paper bag

from under Henry's bed.

"I think I like these better," she said.

She threw one to Mudge

and she threw one to Henry

and she threw one into her own mouth.

"Sometime you'll have to visit *me*,"
said Annie.

"Sure," said Henry.

"Be sure to bring the Frisbee," Annie said.

She looked at Mudge drooling on the bed.

"And be sure to bring Mudge."

The next day Henry and Mudge

said good-bye to Annie.

Mudge gave her another kiss.

This time Annie didn't turn pink.

Henry and Mudge watched

Cousin Annie ride away.

They both couldn't wait to see her again.